Gerry the Giraffe

written by JUNE WOODMAN
and RITA GRAINGE

illustrated by JAMES HODGSON

Gerry had all sorts of problems when he first was taken to the Safari Park because it seemed that he was too tall. However, his height saved the day when the warden's son was missing, and it helped him to round up some poachers who had captured his animal friends. Two delightfully illustrated rhyming stories which will entertain all young children.

First edition

The too-tall giraffe

Ladybird Books Loughborough

In hot and sunny Africa
So many miles away,
A lovely little animal
Was left alone one day.

He seemed to be all legs and neck,
His body was quite small;
His head was very little, too,
It was no size at all.

Escaping from a thunder-storm,
He'd lost his Mum and Dad.
A big tear trickled down his cheek,
He felt so very sad.

Poor Gerry sat alone and cried,
As daylight turned to dark.
A great big lorry rattled up
From the Safari Park.

Out jumped a large and jolly man.
"You're lost. It's plain to see.
I know the very place for you,
So come along with me!"

Then through the still and starry night
The Warden took him home.
"There's plenty here to eat and drink,
You'll have no need to roam."

9

Next day, the Warden's son came out
To see his friends, and play
With Pygmy hippos, lion cubs,
And monkeys small and gay.

He splashed the baby elephant,
And tweaked the monkey's tail.
He tried to climb on Gerry's back,
But all to no avail.

"I cannot reach you," said the boy,
"It's not that I'm too small;
Your legs have grown so very long,
You really are *too* tall."

Poor Gerry tried with all his might
To join in with the rest.
But everything he did went wrong —
He was a perfect PEST!

He looked for tasty tit-bits in
A paw-paw tree nearby.
But he disturbed a hornet's nest,
And DID those hornets fly!

The hornets chased the animals
And all the Warden's men.
They buzzed and stung and zoomed
  about,
Then they buzzed off again.

Quite unconcerned, the young giraffe
Now ambled off to check
The Warden's office where he got
Some wires wrapped round his neck.

The wires were for the radio,
And now it wouldn't work,
Because our Gerry snapped it with
One sudden mighty jerk.

This made the Warden furious.

"I cannot make a call!

We've lost our precious radio

Because you are TOO TALL!"

Then Gerry thought he'd join the rest
Up at the lodge for tea.
But he dragged all the washing down,
A funny sight to see.

He staggered to the windows with
The washing round his neck.
The curtains caught upon his horns.
The house looked such a wreck!

He couldn't get into the room
No matter how he tried;
So nibbled at the roofing thatch
Until the Warden cried,

"He's FAR too tall, he'll have to go,
And here we have the proof.
He's wrecked the house and garden
   and
He's eaten half the roof!"

20

21

22

So sadly Gerry wandered off
Beyond the garden wall.
"Nobody loves me just because
I am so VERY tall!"

"Too Tall! Too tall!" the Warden's cry
Still echoed in his ears.
He didn't see the boy run past,
His eyes were full of tears.

The boy ran past with Monkey's paw
Clutched firmly in his hand.
They dodged out through the Game
  Park fence
To the 'Forbidden Land'.

Poor Gerry thought he'd better leave.
But as he went away —
"My boy is lost. PLEASE look for him!"
He heard the Warden say.

At once there was a hue and cry;
The country was so wild,
That everyone was worried for
The safety of the child.

The Warden and his men spread out
Across the open plain.
The animals were helping too
With all their might and main.

They did their best to find him but,
Because the grass was high,
They missed both Monkey and the
    child,
As they went pushing by.

From down below they couldn't see
The boy's shirt — red and white.
They didn't have the benefit
Of Gerry's extra height.

But *Gerry* saw the runaways.
On guard he waited there,
Until the Warden noticed him,
And found the naughty pair.

So homeward the procession went,
While Gerry, with delight,
Was told by all, "You're NOT too tall.
For us you are JUST RIGHT!"

Gerry leads
the way

One day at the Safari Lodge
The animals were glum.
They couldn't see to left or right
For brushes, paint, and gum.

Spring cleaning at Safari Park
Meant lots of different tasks,
Like mending and repainting all
The shields, and spears, and masks.

"There's nothing much to do round
  here,

Today," the monkey said.

"Let's go to the 'Forbidden Land',

And play out there instead."

So out crept all the animals
On tip-toe, in a row.
The Warden was so busy that
He didn't see them go.

They frolicked through the waving
  grass,
Until they reached the pool.
They paddled, splashed, and drank
  their fill
Of water clear and cool.

The Pygmy hippos made mud-pies,

While Gerry munched at trees.

The lion cubs played hide-and-seek.

The monkeys searched for fleas.

The day wore on. The sun went down.
They all began to feel
That it was time to hurry home
And get their evening meal.

They all set off in single file.
And Gerry, in full sail,
Led Pygmy hippos, lion cubs,
And monkeys at the tail.

But in the dark they lost their way,
And wandered off the track.
They couldn't see the dangers in
The jungle thick and black.

Some wicked men had been at work
And all their traps were set.
The monkeys found themselves
    strung up
Inside a poacher's net.

But that was not the only thing
Those wicked men had done.
For down into a pit, the lions
Tumbled one by one.

And last of all, those wicked men
Had rigged a special trap.
The Pygmy hippos tripped the wire –
The door fell with a SNAP!

Still blithely Gerry trotted on.
He was quite unaware,
That all his friends had fallen foul
Of net and trap and snare.

But when he reached Safari Lodge,
He found himself alone.
The Warden was dismayed when he
Saw Gerry on his own.

''It must be poachers, setting traps
For creatures in the Park.
At day-break we will look for them
But now it is too dark.''

Poor Gerry wandered round the yard,
All lonely and forlorn.
Got paint upon his shoulders, and
A mask hooked on his horn.

40

He was so sad he didn't see
The damage he had done.
''I'll look for them right now!'' he said,
And set off at a run.

He really was quite frightened as
He hurried through the Park.
He didn't like the jungle, and
He didn't like the dark.

But *poachers* like the darkness, for

It hides them from all eyes.

And they came back, with guns and van,

To gather up their prize.

They grabbed the monkeys from the net,

Although they scratched and bit.

They pulled the little lions up

Out of the dreadful pit.

They hauled the hippos from their cage
With a triumphant shout;
But GERRY was behind a bush —
And then the moon came out.

It shone upon the painted mask
High up above the tree.
It scared the poachers half to death.
They all turned round to flee.

One fled into the monkey's net,
One fled into the cage.
The third one fell into the pit —
He fired his gun in rage!

And really that was his mistake.
The Warden heard the shot.
He soon arrived with all his men,
And said, "We've caught the lot!"

"We've caught the straying animals,
We've caught the poachers too!
Our Pygmy hippos, monkeys, cubs,
Won't end up in the zoo."

Again our *too-tall* Gerry led
Them home triumphantly.
The poachers went to prison, *but*
The animals went FREE!

GERRY the GIRAFFE